# Firefighters!

## Speeding! Spraying! Saving!

written by
**Patricia Hubbell**

illustrated by
**Viviana Garofoli**

Amazon Children's Publishing

To Sergio for his love and cooperation—V.G.

Text copyright © 2012 by Patricia Hubbell
Illustrations copyright © 2012 by Amazon Children's Publishing
First Amazon Children's Publishing paperback edition, 2012

Amazon Publishing
Attn: Amazon Children's Publishing
P.O. Box 400818
Las Vegas, NV 89149
www.amazon.com/amazonchildrenspublishing

Library of Congress Cataloging-in-Publication Data
Hubbell, Patricia.
Firefighters! : speeding! spraying! saving! / by Patricia Hubbell ; illustrations by Viviana Garofoli.
p. cm.
Summary: Illustrations and rhyming text celebrate firefighters and what they do.
978-0-7614-5337-6 (hardcover) 978-0-7614-6245-3 (paperback)
[1. Fire fighters–Fiction. 2. Stories in rhyme.]  I. Garófoli, Viviana, ill. II. Title.

PZ8.3.H848Fir 2006
[E]–dc22

2006012989

Book design by Vera Soki

Printed in Malaysia (T)
10 9 8 7 6 5 4 3 2 1

CLANG! CLANG! CLANG!

Firefighters rush! Scurry!
Down the pole. Slide! Hurry!

Put on great big fireproof suits.
Put on helmets, gloves, and boots.

Here comes Spot, the pet Dalmatian,

ready to leave the fire station.

Swing aboard! Hit the gas.

Ladder truck roars, heads out fast.

Sirens screech—Whee-ahh! Whooo!

HHHH!!! WHOOOOOOO!

Pumper truck comes zooming through!

Chief's car races, warning lights flash.

WHEE-AHH! WHEE-AHH! WHEE-AHH! WHOOO!

Cars pull over, engines pass.

Lift the ladders, haul the hose.

Hydrant's open, water flows.

Flames flare up into the sky.

Aim that water, shoot it high.

Crackle! Sizzle! Thunder! Roar!
Swing that hatchet, break the door.

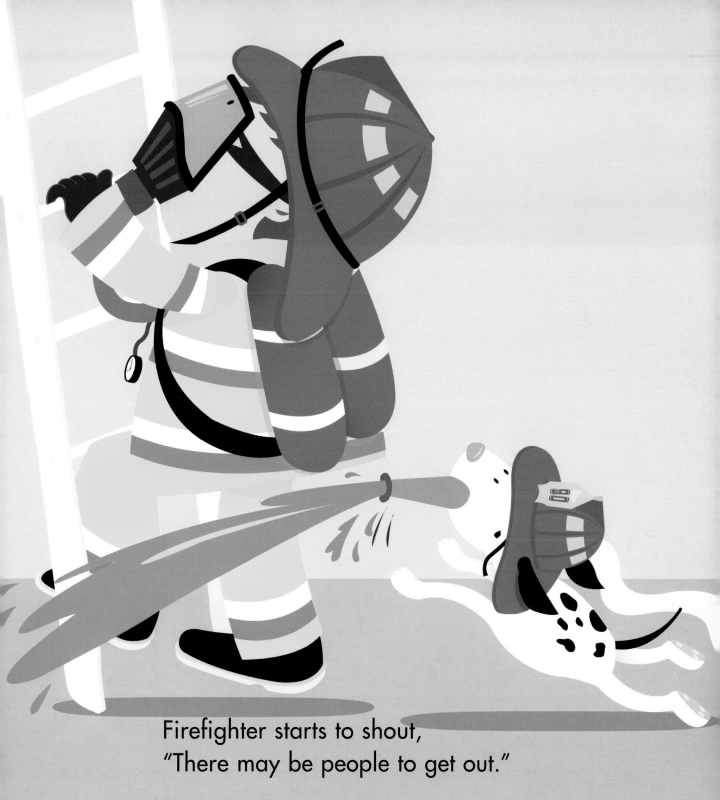

Firefighter starts to shout,
"There may be people to get out."

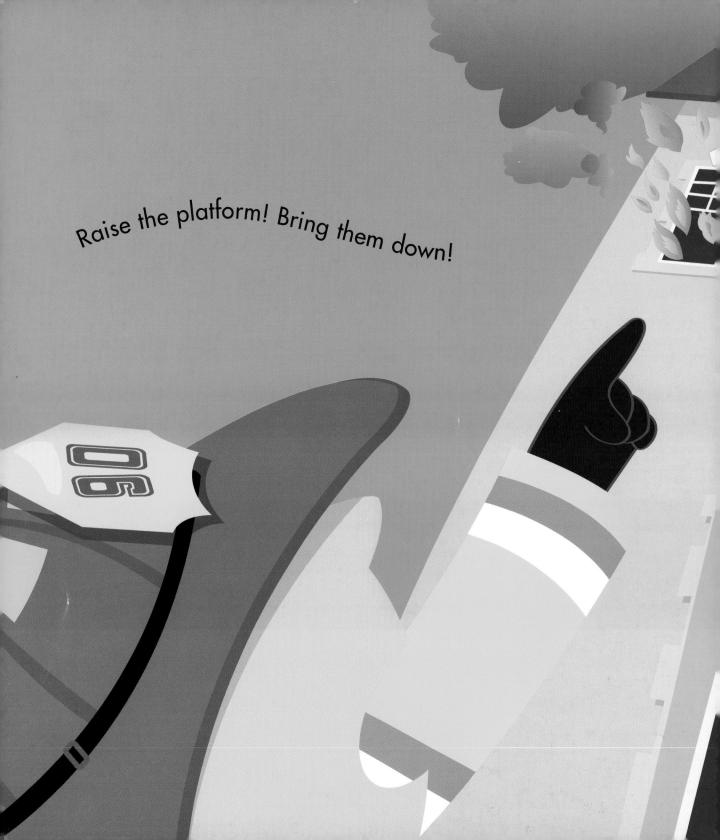

Raise the platform! Bring them down!

Safe and sound on
solid ground.

Hooray! Hooray! Watchers cheer.

Rescue truck is waiting near.

Grab the saws, axes, sledges.
To the roof, walls, and ledges.

Water whooshes, hisses, sprays.
Fire crew has saved the day.

No more danger. Fire's out.
Only ashes swirl about.

Pack the trucks, coil the hose.

Back to town the tired crew goes.

Check equipment, clean each truck.

Clean the clothes of guck and muck.

Rest. Talk. Laugh. Eat.
Spot gets a special treat.

All is quiet. All is still.
Firefighters relax until . . .

CLANG! CLANG! CLANG!